Pattacake, Pattacake, baker's man,
Bake me a cake as fast as you can;
Pat it and prick it and mark it with P,
Put it in the oven for you and for me.

Pattacake, Pattacake, baker's man,
Bake me a cake as fast as you can;
Roll it up, roll it up;
And throw it in a pan!

Pattacake, Pattacake, baker's man.

MR PATTACAKE
and the
MEDIEVAL FEAST

'A feast! A medieval feast!' Mr Pattacake had opened his mail and was now waving a letter in the air enthusiastically. Treacle, his ginger cat, opened one eye lazily, knowing what was coming next.

Sure enough, Mr Pattacake began to do his silly dance, which he always did when he was excited. His big chef's hat wobbled animatedly as he danced around.

Treacle had no idea what the word **MEDIEVAL** meant, but he didn't like the sound of the *evil* part. It reminded him of that rascal cat, Naughty Tortie, who was always teasing him.

Mr Pattacake smiled. He knew exactly what Treacle was thinking. He was good at reading cats' minds – well, at least Treacle's, anyway.

'They're holding a medieval fun day in the sports field,' he said. 'There will be all kinds of games, like jousting and archery - all those fun activities from medieval times, which were a long time ago. They've asked me to do the feast.'

FEAST. Now that was a word that Treacle knew very well, and it was very interesting from his point of view. He knew that it meant food – and lots of it! And when Mr Pattacake made food, there was always something for him to eat.

'I must find out about medieval feasts and make a list,' said Mr Pattacake. He liked making lists and always said that it was the reason why he was so efficient.

He went onto the internet and did a search for medieval feast food. Then he grabbed his pen and a piece of paper, sat down at the table, and began to write.

Finally, he sat back in his chair and sighed.

'Listen, Treacle,' he said, waving his list in the air to get the cat's attention. 'This is what I'm going to make.'

Treacle sat up and listened with interest.

'There'll be potage to start with – that's soup,' he said. 'Then lamb stew with sage and parsley, cheese tarts, pease porridge with onions, and pork and chicken pies. That's the savoury food. Now for the desserts. I'll make crispels – they were a favourite. Not for you, though, Treacle. They're pastries basted in honey, so you won't like them. I'll also make meringue mushrooms, and fruit baked in spices.'

'And…' he paused for effect. 'The **SOLTETIE**.'

There was no reaction from Treacle. He had heard enough to make his mouth water and was therefore not interested in this new word.

'If you're wondering what a soltetie is,' Mr Pattacake went on, ignoring the fact that Treacle was not at all interested, 'it's a surprise dish, or something pretending to be something else. I have a great idea for that!'

Treacle stared hard at Mr Pattacake.

'Of course, I shall be making the chocolate mice, too,' added the chef, knowingly. Chocolate mice were Treacle's favourite!

Treacle smiled his cat's smile, now satisfied.

Mr Pattacake spent a long time preparing the

feast. There would be a lot of people to feed, and medieval food couldn't be hurried, especially the soltetie.

He was so busy that by the time all the food had been prepared, **THREE** of his big white aprons hung to dry on the washing line, whilst Treacle lay in a shady patch under a bush, his little tummy full of scraps.

As usual, there had been a little disaster with the chocolate mice, so he had been a very helpful cat indeed and cleaned it all up (even though chocolate is not good for cats).

When the day of the feast arrived at last, Mr Pattacake loaded all the food into his little yellow van, and he and Treacle set off for the sports field.

It looked wonderful! The children from the local school had handmade and painted all the scenery.

There were castle walls with turrets, a pretend drawbridge, and even a portcullis over the entrance. To one side of the field, long trestle tables were ready for the feast under a big marquee.

On the other side, a trebuchet had been set up, and elsewhere were archery targets and a big sign saying **BIRDS OF PREY DISPLAY.**

Right in the centre of the field was a tower with a window at the top.

'I think that's where the damsel in distress will be rescued by a knight on horseback,' said Mr Pattacake to Treacle, as they stood inside the entrance, looking around in awe.

Treacle kept glancing at the jagged portcullis above them. It was making him very **NERVOUS**.

Mr Pattacake laughed at his expression. 'It's only made out of cardboard, Treacle,' he said, reading the cat's mind.

'Although it does look very realistic. Come on, let's unload the van and start setting the tables.'

'Hello, Mr Pattacake,' said some of the children, who knew him well from parties he had catered for.

They made a fuss over Treacle, too, who rubbed against their legs, purring loudly. He was really going to enjoy the day.

Outside the gate, in a small field at the side, some of the knights in armour were tending to their horses.

They were putting on the saddles and bridles, and also the long fabric drapes which hung down on either side.

Mr Pattacake knew that there was going to be some **JOUSTING**, and he really wished he could have a go. It was something he had always wanted to try. The knights were young people with ponies, and the lances were cardboard tubes, so no one would get hurt.

Mr Pattacake unloaded his little yellow van and then spread paper tablecloths on the tables,

clamping them down securely with plastic clamps
to stop the wind from blowing them away.

Then he put the packs of paper plates and napkins
at one end ready for the diners to help themselves.

They didn't have paper plates and napkins in medieval times, but it would save on the washing up. They would usually have eaten with their fingers in those days, as well as stabbing at the food with their daggers and then eating it off the end. But that seemed a little dangerous, so Mr Pattacake decided that fingers were best – and the napkins would be needed to wipe them.

Pewter goblets had been replaced by plastic cups as they were disposable, and there was a shortage of pewter goblets. There was wine and ale for the grown-ups and squash and cola for the children.

Finally, Mr Pattacake put the food out on big metal trays, still covered with cling film to keep off the flies.

Medieval people did not used to worry too much about flies and germs. In fact, they didn't even know there was any connection between germs and sickness.

As there was no roasting spit or fire, the hot food was kept warm in big electric pots plugged into a long extension lead from a socket in the village hall. Another modern discovery –
ELECTRICITY.

Still, they were trying their best to be as medieval as possible.

Mr Pattacake left the soltetie in the van. That was for later, at the end of the meal.

People had begun to arrive in large numbers and the archery was soon underway, as were the displays of birds of prey.

The sun warmed Mr Pattacake's face as he busied himself at the table, stopping now and again to watch the **ENORMOUS** birds swishing by, and swooping low over the crowd.

There were hawks and eagles and some magnificent owls, and a big crowd had gathered to watch.

Some of the children had put on huge gauntlets and had owls perched on their arms, their immense **CLAWS** gripping their small hands.

Suddenly, there was a commotion around the trebuchet – the giant slingshot that, in medieval times, would have hurled great balls of rock to breach castle walls.

This trebuchet, however, was considerably smaller, since hurling rocks from the sports field might have been a little dangerous.

'MR PATTACAKE!'

A small boy was running towards him, holding a struggling, and very irritated, Treacle in his arms.

'Your cat was asleep in the trebuchet sling and nearly got thrown into the air,' said the boy, breathlessly, as he dumped Treacle onto the ground.

Treacle gave a small shake of annoyance and strutted off. He hated his sleep being disturbed, and the trebuchet sling had been very cosy.

Mr Pattacake smiled at the boy. 'What are you going to use for hurling?' he asked, curiously.

'Well, that's the problem,' said the boy, hopping from one foot to the other in excitement. 'Nobody thought of that. We can't use real rocks like they used to. People will get hurt.'

'No you can't,' said Mr Pattacake. 'But I think I have just the thing.' He bent down and picked up a large sack from the ground and handed it to the boy. 'I had a lot of bread rolls left over from a party the other day and they're stale now so we can't eat them. They will make good missiles, don't you think?'

The boy nodded enthusiastically, taking the sack from Mr Pattacake and dragging it towards the trebuchet.

When the trebuchet started up there were times when the missiles went astray, but being hit by a bread roll was not such a disaster.

38

When the food was ready, Mr Pattacake banged a
BIG GONG to get everyone's attention.

He didn't know whether or not they had gongs in
medieval times, but he'd bought it at a car boot sale
and had been waiting for the perfect opportunity
to bang it. This seemed like a good occasion, and it
certainly got everyone's attention.

Having worked up an appetite, people began to form a queue and help themselves to food.

The damsel in distress (although she wasn't in distress yet) had come to eat first so that she could climb back up into her tower to be rescued by the knight. She looked lovely, Mr Pattacake thought, with her long blonde hair and wearing a long, white dress.

She tucked into her food heartily in case, he surmised, she wasn't rescued for a long time.

The knights, too, having prepared their horses, lined up to eat.

'**GADZOOKS!**' said one when he saw the tables laden with food. After that, the word seemed to be infectious as they all kept saying it.

The only ones who didn't eat were the acrobats, who were to entertain the diners along with the minstrels, so Mr Pattacake put some food away for them to have later.

When everyone was seated, the minstrels came out to play their recorders and flutes, and even Treacle was amongst them, playing his lute. He loved to play that old instrument, which was just right for medieval times.

Then came the acrobats – children from the gym club – who did forward rolls and back flips, and all sorts of amazing manoeuvres, much to the delight of the crowd, and especially the mums and dads.

After the display, they all came and sat down to eat, along with the minstrels. Treacle was even allowed a chair to himself, so he was very careful with his table manners, although in medieval times they had none at all.

They used to eat with their hands, and throw the scraps that they didn't want onto the floor, as well as belching loudly when they had finished.

They would slurp and gulp their drinks and would generally eat **GREEDILY**.

This feast, however, was a little more polite, although everyone did enjoy forgetting about their table manners once in a while.

Soon it was time for the desserts, and the soltetie.

Mr Pattacake went to his van and opened the back doors. Then he reached in and carefully pulled out a heavy tray, which had something on it covered with a cloth.

There was complete silence as he placed it on a table; everyone was intrigued to see what it was. With a flourish, like a magician doing a magic trick, Mr Pattacake whipped off the cover.

A **GASP** went up from the crowd. On the tray was a beautiful **DRAGON** moulded from sugar. Its scales glistened in the sunlight and its orange eyes sparkled realistically. It had a long tail, and was holding its head up with its mouth open.

But Mr Pattacake wasn't finished. He took a box of matches out of his apron pocket, struck one, and held it to the dragon's open mouth.

With a loud noise, roaring **FLAMES** shot out, making everyone back away, nervously, until they saw that they were only little flames, coming out from a thin tube inside the dragon's mouth.

Then the whole crowd clapped, and Mr Pattacake bowed in acknowledgement, pleased that his idea had been received so well.

He was so happy that he did his silly dance to the music of the minstrels (including Treacle), who had picked up their instruments again. The excitement was infectious, and soon everyone was up and dancing to the jovial music.

Meanwhile, at the birds of prey table, a big barn owl had spotted something interesting on the food table. It was not the dragon soltetie, but some little brown creatures with their tails waving in the breeze.

The owl spread its great wings and took off to get a closer look.

The creatures looked like **MICE!**

It was his lucky day. So many mice all together in one place! He swooped down on the table and stood there, his wings flapping slowly as he balanced on the rim of a big bowl, and dipped his beak forward to pick up a chocolate mouse.

The draught from the owl's flapping wings caused a paper napkin to lift up from the table and flutter in front of the dragon's mouth, where the small flames were still flickering out.

With one little flare, the paper napkin caught fire and floated up into the air towards the cardboard scenery, trailing smoke behind it. There it settled, and a little flame licked at the scenery hungrily – and then set it alight.

'**FIRE!**' one of the archers shouted, running towards the now blazing scenery.

The music stopped. The people stopped dancing and gazed in horror at the burning scenery.

But the archer who first saw the fire had pushed the piece of scenery to the ground and stamped on it several times.

Then he poured a jug of ale over it, putting out the flames immediately. So no real harm was done.

The damsel in distress, however, was still frightened. She had seen the fire from the top of the tower, where she was waiting to be rescued by a knight on horseback. She was so scared of her tower burning down, that instead of climbing back down the ladder to the ground, she just hung out of the window shouting, '**HELP!**'

Where was the knight who was meant to rescue her? Mr Pattacake wondered. He looked around but couldn't see him anywhere. But Mr Pattacake knew what he had to do. He sprinted to the tower and began to climb up the side. The tower had been made with a kind of ladder built into the side to make the climb easier, but nevertheless, it wasn't easy after all that dancing and eating.

Finally, Mr Pattacake reached the damsel, who was really in great distress by now, and held out his hand to her.

'Climb out and follow me down,' he said, trying to calm her down. 'You'll be all right.'

The damsel did so, and as they climbed down the tower, the crowd below cheered them on. All except the knight who was meant to have rescued her. He had turned up now, on his horse, and was looking very cross and very unknightlike, with a pout on his face.

While all this was going on, Treacle had spotted the owl, who was still trying to steal the chocolate mice. There was something familiar about that owl and the way it furtively looked round with its big round eyes, before pecking at the mice. It reminded

Treacle of that mischievous tortoiseshell cat, Naughty Tortie, who was always lurking around to see what she could get her paws on.

Seeing that the mice were not real, however, the owl flew back to its owner, disappointed. But Treacle was still watching the table when another movement caught his attention. A dark, furry face appeared above the table just where the owl had been, and stealthily climbed up to sniff the chocolate mice. But these didn't interest her this time. There was better food to be had, which was more to a cat's liking.

Treacle let out a loud yowl and sprang forward, his lute falling to the ground as he tore towards the table, bravely chasing Naughty Tortie as she began to creep towards the delicious food.

Mr Pattacake had by now seen the damsel safely to the ground and made sure she was no longer in distress. He knew what Treacle was saying and ran towards the table, too.

'**SHOO!**' he shouted, flapping his hands. 'Get away, Naughty Tortie. We must not have cats on the table.' Naughty Tortie eyed Mr Pattacake and Treacle and then scuttled away, disappointed.

Mr Pattacake switched off the dragon's flame
and began to cut the soltetie up into pieces for the
people to eat.

The damsel (no longer in distress) was the first to try some, along with her knight, who was still a bit cross that he had not rescued her. However, tasting the delicious sugary dragon treat soon put a smile on his face, and another '**GADZOOKS!**'

Mr Pattacake was hailed a **HERO**.

'How can we thank you?' asked the archer, who had organised the medieval fun day. 'You provided a wonderful feast including a spectacular soltetie dragon, and you also rescued the damsel from the tower. You must be rewarded!'

'Well,' said Mr Pattacake, feeling a bit awkward. 'I've always wanted to have a go at jousting.'

'Then you shall,' exclaimed the archer, happy to grant Mr Pattacake's request as he looked around for a suitable knight. 'Sir Robert! Will you lend Mr Pattacake your horse and lance?'

Sir Robert, who had the largest horse, brought it round and helped Mr Pattacake into the saddle. His big chef's hat wobbled unsteadily and he looked quite comical sitting up on the horse, still wearing his big white apron.

The crowd followed Mr Pattacake to the side of
the field where the jousting was taking place.

There he waited at one end, while another knight on horseback waited at the other, on the opposite side of the rope fence.

A signal was given, and both horsemen galloped forward towards each other at full speed, lances held in front of them at the ready.

CRASH! The lances clashed as they passed each other.

Mr Pattacake was really enjoying himself now. He turned at the end and galloped back to challenge his opponent once again. But his horse had other ideas. He was fed up with galloping up and down all morning, and he could almost smell the bale of hay in his stable. So, instead of stopping and turning at the end of the jousting fence, he just kept going towards the edge of the field and the way home.

Mr Pattacake was not an experienced rider, in fact, he had only ever ridden a horse a couple of times, and that was when he was much younger. He was therefore unable to control the horse once it had made up its mind.

Now it was Mr Pattacake's turn to shout for help as the horse sped up.

But he was going so fast that no one could help him. Fortunately, there was no fence around the field, so Mr Pattacake was spared having to cope with jumping over it.

The horse clattered onto the road with Mr Pattacake holding on tightly. His big chef's hat flew straight off his head and landed in a field of cows.

Curiously, they crowded round it, but finding it of no interest, they trod it into the mud.

Mr Pattacake and the horse had reached the farm where it lived and cantered in through the open gate towards the stable. (You should always close farm gates, but luckily this time someone had left it open.)

The stable door, however, was shut, and it was only at the last minute that the horse noticed. It skidded to a sudden stop, but Mr Pattacake did not.

He flew out of the saddle and landed, softly, in a heap of horse manure.

The horse **WHINNIED** as Mr Pattacake stumbled to his feet and brushed himself down.

'Are you saying sorry?' asked the chef in good humour. He wasn't angry. The jousting had certainly been more exciting than he had anticipated, although he probably wouldn't be jousting again anytime soon.

He was about to open the stable door to let the horse in, when Sir Robert, the horse's young owner, came running up, panting.

'Are you all right, Mr Pattacake?' he asked, looking worried.

'I think so,' said the chef. He tried to smile as the ghastly smell of the manure invaded his nostrils. 'I smell a bit, and I've lost my hat somewhere.'

'I'll get you a new one,' said the young knight, gallantly. He was horrified that Mr Pattacake had got into such a mess. 'I should have warned you that Thunder was a strong-willed horse.'

'And I should stick to cooking instead of jousting,' said Mr Pattacake, chuckling.

After herding Thunder into his stable, they went back to the sports field where everyone was pleased to see that the chef was unharmed. Mr Pattacake began clearing up the remainder of the feast and putting aside some leftover food for his tea, as well as for Treacle – and for Naughty Tortie. He'd had a feeling she was skulking around nearby, and he couldn't help but feel a little affection towards her, despite her naughty ways.

Well, it had certainly been an exciting day! **GADZOOKS!**